One Chance: 20 Short Stories with a Plot Twist and Moral Lesson

Rowan Knight

Published by 22 Lions Bookstore, 2016.

Table of Contents

Title Page

One Chance: 20 Short Stories with a Plot Twist and Moral Lesson
By Rowan Knight

Published by 22 Lions Bookstore and Publishing House

About the Publisher

About the 22 Lions Bookstore:
        www.22Lions.com
Facebook.com/22Lions
Twitter.com/22lionsbookshop
Instagram.com/22lionsbookshop
Pinterest.com/22lionsbookshop

Introduction

Do people have second chances in their life? And what is the price we pay for past mistakes? How important is karma? This compilation of short stories, inspired on real life events and people, intends to show how were so many individuals able to redirect their path towards a more fulfilling outcome, and in doing so, found love, happiness and confidence in themselves. The stories presented here are inspirational and motivational, and intend to promote a renewed sense of faith in oneself. These are stories that show us the best way of dealing with spiritual struggles and teach also how to make difficult decisions at any given moment.

The Chicken Bird Can Fly

There was once a woman in her early thirties who had been abandoned by many boyfriends. Her self-esteem was low and she was often feeling ugly and useless. She nevertheless dreamed of an opportunity to change her life and anxiously waited for it to come in the form of love.

One day, she met a guy, felt connected to him, and then fell in love with him. She said he was her lucky Bluebird and he called her his Chickenbird, because as he observed, she didn't seem to have enough self-esteem to "fly in life".

What she couldn't understand is why he liked her so much, even thought he was always making fun of her weaknesses. She had never experienced love, and so, in order to prove to herself that everything was an illusion, that he wasn't loving her but would eventually leave her just like anyone else did, she started provoking and criticizing him. And yet, every time this occurred, and he was about to leave her, she felt as if losing something valuable, reason why she would try to talk him back to her life. Inside herself, still survived a strong and painful contradiction between fear of abandonment and a deep will to live, to feel alive. And she didn't know what to do. Chickenbird just couldn't accept happiness. Sadness and self-pity had become an important part of her character.

The quarrels in what was meant to be a love story persisted for a long time and, in one of such days, she even admitted why she was being so mean to him:

— "I can't understand why you love me. The other men I have been with before sent me love messages but you don't. You don't even ever call me. I'm the one always calling you. Besides, I'm fat, I have a big head, I'm ugly and I'm stupid. I don't even know why you are still with me."

Bluebird looked at her in bewilderment as paused to meditate on her words. He then answered:

— "Look, if I am with you, it is because I can see things that you can't. You're not fat. You just have this tendency to dress large clothes and walk around like a fat person would because you think you're that kind of woman. You don't have a big head either; you merely enjoy making your hair look like a bird's nest because you believe it makes you seem stylish, even though it actually makes your head appear much bigger than normal. And you're not ugly as well, but you do dress and behave as if you were. You're also not stupid; you just think you are and convinced yourself of that."

Chickenbird was speechless and reflected profoundly on his words. But in order to prove himself, in the following days, Bluebird taught her how to dress better and persuaded her to change hairstyle. He also taught her how to walk, talk and behave differently.

A few months later, Chickenbird went to meet her friends.

— "Wow, you're so beautiful", they said in amazement.

— "What happened to you?", they continued asking, completely astonished with her new appearance.

Chickenbird, herself, could't believe that, for the first time ever, her friends were jealous of her looks. They kept saying that she was the most beautiful in the group and that the guy responsible for this was certainly unique. They became very curious in knowing who this man was, for he had the potential to make any woman look beautiful.

In that same evening after the encounter, Chickenbird went back home full of joy and told Bluebird how appreciated she was.

— "I now know that you love me, even though you have never said it, or used the same words other men have told me, because you have taught me how to love myself and that is only possible by loving me as I am".

Bluebird smiled with a sense of pride for her.

— "You're no Chickenbird anymore", he replied. — "You can fly now. As a matter of fact, by noticing the many men starring at you while you walk outside, I can also confirm that you're more than a bird now. You have turned into an eagle", he told her, while keeping a nurturing smile on his face. And, at that moment, she couldn't hold her tears and started crying.

— "I've done many facial and body treatments during my whole live and never changed as much as now."

ONE CHANCE

Chickenbird couldn't understand what happened but, in his wisdom, Bluebird knew very well what he had done and tried to help her accept this experience.

— "The power of real love and true happiness becomes a glow of energy that changes every single cell of your body and mind, and this is something that nobody can ever tell you or even lie about, as you can feel it, and that is how you know who loves you."

Indeed, it was real love that Chickenbird was experiencing, but she couldn't identify with the Eagle side of her — the new self. She still doubted the results and questioned if this man was in love with her new or old self. And she still couldn't fully identify with the new appearance. She never felt so amazingly well before, the feeling was overwhelming, and everything seemed too good to be true, so good that it made her feel uncomfortable and confused as well.

This confusion would soon end, as her former boyfriend, a businessman from Australia, was visiting the city where they lived, and insisted on seeing her. The scars had not yet healed, she still had some feelings for him despite being betrayed and abandoned. And Chickenbird ended up succumbing to his insistences and threats, mostly because she wanted to know if she still had feelings for him; and wanted to know too if Bluebird was just an illusion by comparing those emotions that she felt for both. Within her confusion and indecisions, she believed this was an opportunity to clear things inside her mind. And so, she accepted to see him.

This secret, however, made Bluebird realize that something had changed in his relationship. He was wise beyond what most could see, had sharp instincts too, and his gut feeling was telling him that something was terribly wrong. Just as he could see beauty inside Chickenbird, and bring it out of her, he could also perceive a defense mechanism and betrayal, and knew how to confront her about it to get the truth out.

When succumbing to the persistence and sharpness of the questions, Chickenbird dropped tears and confessed everything.

— "Yes, I went to see him. I didn't know what to do. I can't handle the feelings you awaken in me. I never felt like this before. I wanted to know if I was still in love with him. And I wasn't. In fact, I didn't feel anything with him anymore, apart from repulse and disgust. I love you know. I'm sure I love only you."

Her confession was very sincere and apologetic but Bluebird felt deeply hurt and betrayed by her doubts. Despite her insistence in saying that she didn't have sex with her ex-boyfriend, the fact remained that she did went to see him in order to clarify her feelings, and knowing it was enough for Bluebird to lose trust on her. Chickenbird could see that in his face too and was very afraid to lose her true love. She wouldn't accept the breakup and even threatened him that she would commit suicide if he abandoned her. She actually became haunted by her own mistake, terrified about the idea of losing Bluebird, and made sure to be always home when he arrived from work.

Months had passed and the problem seemed forgotten. Meanwhile, Chikenbird had a business trip and, when she was abroad, Bluebird sent a final message before vanishing from her life.

— "I'm sorry but I can't continue on suffering with you and living a lie. I rather be alone than love someone that hurts me. Goodbye!"

Chickenbird couldn't believe this message was for real. She insisted on calling him, sent messages and visited the last city where they had been together but couldn't find him. He had changed country and was never to be seen again.

Unable to cope with the pain of losing the man that gave her a second chance in life, the only man who truly loved her and, more than that, the only man who made her love herself, she lost hope. From that day on, Chickenbird spent her mornings, and for many years, looking from her apartment window, thinking about the happy moments they spent together and knowing that her wings had been forever lost. No other man was ever able to replace her beautiful memories and stop her nostalgic tears. Every new partner she had remembered her of Bluebird, and she cried every time they kissed or had sex. Everyone made her remember the mistake she did and for the rest of her life.

The Witch's Daughter

Daughter of a popular village sorcerer in the south of France, Juliette seemed to be born from a curse. Since an early age that she had been demonstrating a strong sexual desire far beyond normal. And at the beginning, life seemed to her as if it was all about just having fun, pleasure and entertainment at her feet. She would seduce and invite men to her house, trying all types of excuses to stimulate their interest, and while still a teenager, have sex with as many as possible. Later in life, she would start going to clubs and bars, to diversify her options. She had sex with married men, participated in orgies, joined couples, had lesbian sex,...; Juliette would literally participate in everything she could, out of curiosity, or simply interest, and because she was also addicted to sex in general.

When things went out of control, she tried seeing a psychiatrist. But ended up seducing him too, and falling into the temptation of having sex with him. It was at that point that she realized she couldn't help herself, because, quite simply, sex was a strong impulse in every human being, that she uncontrollably felt the need to stimulate. And with every conquest, came a sense of pride, of rejuvenating strength, replacing her very low self-esteem. These wild adventures represented more than sex to her. They were as an exciting game, which she loved to play. And with every new heart possessed, either using her intelligence, looks, or spells learned from her mother, her pride increased furthermore and fueled a sensation of power coming from within.

Juliette could have any man she wanted, for she was extremely attractive, feminine and seductive, which altogether empowered her with an irresistible magnetism that was almost impossible to resist. But Juliette was also still sixteen, when realizing that her skills to seduce anyone would come with a price that would cost her reputation and cause much pain. Regularly and brutally beaten by a shamed and frustrated mother, that had gone mad in trying to find ways to raise Juliette, with or without spells, Juliette knew that she had to runaway from home in order to continue being who she was. That thought was reinforced when she was brutally beaten by a group of school girls for having sex with their boyfriends.

She was fearing for her life, and suffering with the consequences of her actions. And after the school administration had a meeting with her mother about it, she decided to put her own daughter in a psychiatric hospital. And yet, Juliette would not stay there for long. She seduced one of psychiatrists into having sex with her, took his keys, and when he was sleeping, she escaped. But being as fast and agile as a professional athlete wasn't enough. She always ended up being caught, either when climbing over the gates of the hospital or afterwards.

Juliette had to think more strategically to be able to escape. And so, she convinced one of the psychiatrists to take her to his home, so that they could be in a close relationship. He changed her diagnosis in order to bring her to his apartment under the condition that she would never leave until a cure was made possible.

This man had fallen in love, but kept her locked in the house during the entire time she was there, as he knew perfectly well that Juliette was very sick.

Juliette, however, who was always thinking about ways to escape, managed to access the codes of his credit cards and then buy a plane ticket to London. When he wasn't at home, she made her move, by escaping through the window using bed sheets as a rope. A taxi was already waiting for her. She was finally heading to her freedom.

She managed to arrive in London by herself, and now Juliette was truly alone, feeling abandoned, absolutely humiliated, but also free to be who she truly is and without anyone stopping her.

Her pride took the shape of resentment and revenge, and that's when she decided to push her boundaries one step further. With the mental expertise of a vampire that had lived for hundreds of years, the sweet eyes of Juliette could easily deceive anyone into anything, even the brightest. She was only a 16yo teenager, but extremely attractive and captivating. She didn't have much money for a room, but always persuaded any hotel receptionist to offer her a corner where to sleep, a small place, quite often his own. Juliette didn't mind that, and didn't mind paying for it with sex either. But she knew she had to solve her situation quickly. And while trying to find a job, she felt lucky with an opportunity that she found to become a baby-sitter in the mansion of a rich family.

She became a baby-sitter to many families, for she was usually fired for either rarely sleeping at home, or for being caught sleeping with the father of the children by his own wife.

She then decided to try having a more stable job by combining her attributes and desires, and that's how she ended up working at a porn shop. Many clients would often invite her for orgies and she denied none. In fact, she felt that it was just too easy now to get all the sex she wanted. It felt normal too. As normal as the next step she would take.

London was still a very expensive city for her and the job wasn't paying well enough. So Juliette decided to become a prostitute. She would place ads in the newspaper and also visit local pubs to seduce men to her room. She would prefer the second option, as she wanted to choose who to sleep with, and she was still young and attractive enough to do exactly that.

Most of the clients had no idea whatsoever that they were sleeping with a minor and didn't care either, even if they found. Juliette was irresistible, and the way she had sex, was like a snake, it was as if she knew exactly all the right moves and positions for each man. And she enjoyed that, she enjoyed studying them, to know how far she could go with each one, and how fast she could make them reach climax.

Juliette went far very quickly, from merely wanting to survive to being extremely wealthy. Her young appearance, petite and very sexy body, sex hunger, and wit, made her addictive to men. So much she was irresistible, that she took the next stage, when being regularly invited to the richest parties in London. She would become the mistress and lover of many important politicians and businessmen. And the ones she liked best, due to all the luxuries they offered her and travels around the world, she would pick for a relationship.

Life couldn't be better. Juliette had it all — the finest hotels, parties, and wealth. She also had handsome men with all of that — everything she ever imagined possible— proposing marriage. But the demon inside Juliette was restless. She could not be monogamous, she always got bored easily, and her hormones and endless thoughts would drive her insane. She cheated in her relationships, and she would often escape from the house just to have sex with any random guy she could find outdoors, either in a nearby bar, shop, or even in the street. She had a way of captivating men's attention with her eyes, and the ones she selected would fall for it easily.

The need to hide her behaviors would then turn to drama, and the drama in the relationship to more guilt; and when the opportunity appeared, as it always did, she would move on to someone else that could offer her the same luxury.

At this point in life, Juliette had more money than she could spend, and she could pick any man she wanted too. However, she couldn't settle with anyone. And that's when she decided to simply assume that none of her relationships would ever last.

Knowing this, she always planned ahead, and stole from her partners, by transferring their money to her bank accounts without them knowing it. She was very skillful at discovering passwords, including when they thought she wasn't looking. She knew how to deceive them well.

Instead of focusing on relationships, Juliette now focused on sex. But then, she started fearing for her life. Detectives were being hired to stalk her and investigate her. The local police also had several reports on her, even though not enough evidence yet to put her in jail. She was already in her thirties by now, and had no qualifications to do anything else, but hooking up with rich men and being offered to live in their house. So she falsified her Resume and created a PhD diploma, and moved to China in order to become a lecturer. And that was the perfect disguise. No law could catch her there.

Juliette was extremely clever but a mirror would not lie. She saw herself turning old, losing the attractiveness she once had. Suddenly, Juliette felt empty too, without any emotional attachments, without anyone to love. The once external struggles were made internal. But she thought that it would be as easy to change herself as when changing anyone else. Juliette thought that she could purify her soul and erase her painful sense of guilt with a true love. And that's when she decided to use what she had learned from her mother, when watching her work with clients, to make a spell that would prove to be one of the strongest she ever did. The ritual performed, intended to attract love in its purest form, a man that would love her unconditionally, a person that she would also fall in love with, to replace her negative karma with a positive one.

ONE CHANCE

In front of a lighted candle, and hours before taking the plane to China, she made it happen, explicitly writing her wish on a piece of a paper and repeating the phrase like a mantra.

— "I will find a good man and he will rescue me with love".

She repeated this with all her heart, taking this mantra deep into her soul. And the spell was so powerful that such man was pulled out of his country with an unexpected job offer he couldn't refuse to become a lecturer in China, and after being fired from his previous job. He took the plane from Madrid to Shanghai and, on arrival at the University, there she was, waiting for him already.

He felt hypnotized by her eyes, but she wasn't sure he was the one. After all, she did the spell thinking about the emotions she wished to feel, but expecting someone older than her, and not ten years younger. Even when Juliette started to feel something inside of her during their conversation, she kept asking herself inside her mind:

— "Is this real love or merely the effect of a strong spell?"

Nonetheless, she couldn't help but notice the fact that she was falling in love too fast and for the first time in her life. She felt weak and powerless, and didn't know how to handle this. Her ankles and legs would often weaken in his presence, and many times she literally fell on the floor or seemed clumsy at the dinner table and in front of everyone, as if she was only three years old and using a fork for the first time. This man made her feel nervous and small, and she found herself struggling for her lost pride. She did try to resist him for a while because he wasn't rich and powerful like all the others she had been with before; he was actually very honest, emphatic and humble, and could easily see her tricks and masks, including when she was lying. But instead of getting angry about it, he would mock her, because he could see that she was merely pretending to be a wise adult while actually acting like a small and immature child.

Apart from not being the type of man she imagined, a man she could control and manipulate, to gain either profit or a better reputation, he was also immune to her tricks. Apart from love, there was really nothing else to gain from this relationship. Juliette was losing her pride, confidence, ability to lie, potential to control, and basically everything she was made comfortable with, everything that was part of who she truly was, or at least the mask she had built for herself. She was losing that mask, her whole fake identity, and experiencing true love with him, as two soulmates. And this scared her tremendously.

That was when the demonic forces took over her mind with a stronger intent. Because, to make everything harder, this man had a strong religious background and was not giving up on his love, no matter how many problems she brought to his life. And Juliette realized what it is to surrender to another soul, because she started to be afraid of losing him, while also being afraid of loving him and lose herself along the way. In other words, Juliette was realizing what it is to be human.

The experience led her to the perception of something she had never seen before, and that was moral and empathy, the fundamental conditions to experience human love. She noticed also the importance of commitment, honesty and caring for someone that love implied; and this increasing consciousness, plus the notion of ethics, terrified her. All of her sins were coming to the surface to haunt her, and at night she was always having nightmares, either related to the past to or to this man.

Juliette felt pressured between choosing to give up on her pride and secrets to fall in love with the heart of this man, and the perpetuation of her pride and lust, by cheating on him with other men.

She believed that she could keep on having both things: her pride and the love of another person. After all, the spell was made already and was working. Therefore, while persuading him to marry her, she continually flirted with strangers and slept with other men, including their own colleagues. Then, as he lost trust for her, and refused to marry her, she convinced herself that this wasn't the man she had been waiting for and gave up on him, abandoned him and runaway with one of such colleagues she had been having sex with behind his back.

This time, however, the cards of life were against her. Merely three months later, the adventure had ended. She was the one being cheated and abandoned. And, while not being able to handle the pain, Juliette desperately tried to recover her previous lover, the one she couldn't forget. But it was too late for that. The spell, broken by her behaviors, wouldn't work again. Besides, this man wouldn't allow himself to be controlled for loving a woman that had broken his heart into pieces.

Juliette realized she had committed the worse act against herself and had lost a chance to be rescued with love, an opportunity to receive mercy for her past. And, as if this wasn't enough, her own spell, by being destroyed by her own deliberate actions, took the form of resentful spirits, which came with a vengeance and destroyed her appearance by stealing vital energy from her, making her look twenty years older and shortening her life span. Her health was quickly deteriorating and she was vomiting all the time. Indeed, this time, Juliette had hurt the wrong man. Her irresponsible actions and spells, on the other hand, made her realize that nothing in life, and especially not even a human being, is immune to one's own evilness.

Unable to be with the only person she loved and while feeling that she had destroyed the only chance to solve her mental disease, and erase her past of madness, she started drinking more. It didn't took long for her addiction to take over her, namely, when her horrible appearance made it nearly impossible to find anyone to have sex with. Due to alcoholism and sex with the most ugly and disgusting men willing to be with her, she became bulimic too. Her madness became difficult to control; she would easily change from flirting with students in her classes to violent reactions when facing rejection, and that's when she couldn't keep a job anymore in China. She then took a job offer as a teacher in Switzerland and tried to live a more isolated life since then. She still has sex on a regular basis with many of her students but, now in her 50s, life just isn't the same for Juliette as it once was, and never was her true love forgotten.

The Personal Bodyguard

Rose was abandoned by her parents when she was still a young child, and ended up being raised by her grandparents. She always felt too small to deal with her life and too undeserving to accept it as well, and this until she was in her thirties. The trauma from her childhood never vanished.

One day a chance appeared to change everything and recreate a new future for herself. She was offered a partnership in a business. The opportunity represented a way to rebuild her self-esteem. Nonetheless, other problems came her way too. Clients didn't trust her and employers didn't respect her, all because she didn't show enough confidence.

She shared this issue with her boyfriend, who often accompanied in business trips to protect her, as well as the fact that she couldn't sleep properly at night because of it and was having many nightmares related to failing in exams.

As a kickboxing instructor, he suggested that she should start practicing this sport to build confidence. Rose was too afraid to get hurt and refused but he insisted. Once she started the classes, he immediately realized the main problem: she didn't have determination, was always ready to quit, insisted on self-judging her performance as weak and pathetic, and kept repeating that she wasn't good enough. And so, he decided to use kickboxing as a way to make her believe the opposite, to rebuild her self-esteem. He convinced her in believing in herself by forcing her to do what she couldn't do for herself and by repeating the exact opposite words that she was saying out loud. This practice helped her gain trust and, later on, the nightmares disappeared. Her clients and employees also started respecting her more, and the business went back on track with a very good outcome. She was making much more money than before, and everything seemed to flow extremely well.

However, she couldn't understand how kickboxing helped her, so the boyfriend explained that, the nightmares related to doing an exam, were related to the need to confront certain emotions and attitudes, namely, lack of confidence, lack of self-control, lack of discipline, fear for the future, and so on.

She still doubted the explanation, so he continued:

— "The training helped in developing qualities needed for business because those dreams were related to things that you need to develop in yourself in order to achieve your goals. Now you know why you had them. You were not ready for the "exam" and the dreams were warnings about it. And yet, seems to me that the exam was not about knowledge, as you probably assumed, but instead characteristics in your personality".

Thanks to his words, Rose realized even more things about herself now, such as that she should stop saying: "I'm going to be bankrupt"; and noticed that she should say instead: "I must be more persistent and hard working". Instead of saying, "I don't make enough money", she should actually repeat, "I must get more money"; And finally, she should replace, "I'm lazy", with "I must concentrate on my efforts".

She basically realized that she had to replace her excuses with mental training while seeing the challenges as opportunities to develop herself.

— "You're not punching, kicking or doing business", he said to her, one more time. — "You're learning how to live the life you want", he added.

Rose realized that her boyfriend was right, but decided to take the lesson one step ahead from what she should, and became a very aggressive person, by imposing herself on others, including on her boyfriend, with shouts and punches every time they had disagreements. The situation shifted from one extreme to the other. But this man didn't like to see her shouting and being aggressive towards him, as he didn't believe in aggression either, and surely didn't want a relationship like that. As a result, he refused to keep traveling with her to protect her in her business trips.

She didn't understood the purpose of his lessons and eventually confused confidence with the ability to suppress others. From victim, she had turned into an aggressor. And still convinced of her own power to use aggression on others, Rose persisted with this idea, didn't contact him anymore to apologize, didn't thought that she would need him as a bodyguard either, and decided to move on with her life and try to find a new boyfriend.

ONE CHANCE

One day, when traveling to south America to a business meeting, she was robbed outside the train station by two women, resisted with shoutings and punches but was severely beaten and stabbed to death.

21

The Hidden Path

Lack of job opportunities were getting too common and Peter, despite his Masters degree, couldn't find a job, no matter how hard he would try. In fact, his luck seemed to go downwards, for not even a relationship he could keep. And these challenges, at a psychological and emotional level, each one on their own turn, was troubling him day and night up to the level of despair. At one point he couldn't even fall a sleep at night, troubled with worries, and he would wake up exhausted too. And so he prayed for answers. The answers came when one day he received an email with a job offer in Thailand. It was surprising, but, on the other hand, he didn't even have enough money in his bank account to buy the plane ticket.

Days later another miracle happened with a phone call:

— "Hi Peter, we are calling you from the bank because you are on a list of clients to whom we wish to offer a loan as part of a special promotion we are currently having. You don't need enough funds in your account or financial guarantees to get it. You only have to accept it or deny it."

Peter couldn't believe what he was hearing. It seemed like an opportunity fallen from the sky. And for that reason, he knew he couldn't say no. He took the loan, and soon after, took three flights to arrive at his destination.

Almost immediately, upon arrival, he noticed several challenges, namely the cultural gap that he had to overcome and the language barrier. He also felt that his knowledge wasn't really going through, as the students weren't paying attention whenever he addressed more personal issues. The lack of attention and disrespect he got in the classroom, led him to write during his non-working hours about everything nobody wanted to hear. He continued doing this for the following five years of his life.

That recognition never came, and he wouldn't succumb to the hypocrisy that was expected from him either. And so, he just kept writing more, and more, and more. Even when he was fired, he would rather focus on his writing, instead of searching for a job. He knew he would always find one if he just kept himself focused on his goal.

As the years passed, he kept getting more depressed, and then sick, but the number of books written had also increased. He had now more than one hundred. He also had several relationships, but none would be enough to distract him from his goal. Whenever a relationship failed, he would simply write more. Whenever he was depressed, he would again, write more. And when writing became more important than expecting anything else in life, when writing replaced hope, hope arrived, for sales picked up really fast. He had turned into a popular author, and reporters were constantly calling him for interviews.

He didn't expect that, and so he pondered for a while about it. He had a stable job but wasn't happy. His book sales kept increasing, and that was his chance to do whatever he wanted with his life. And that's when he realized: We all die but few live.

He then decided to take responsibility for his fate, and quit his job. All of his students laughed simultaneously when he said he would not teach anymore because he had decided to become a full-time writer. They couldn't believe. And yet, that's exactly what he did.

He then booked a plane ticked to Poland, where he was told the most beautiful women live, and traveled between cities, before finding his future wife, with whom he would experience true love as never before. They got married within months, and had three children form that marriage.

His success as an author kept growing and he finally got the respect and admiration he deserved.

The Meaning Behind Zero

Helen was on her first year of college when she received the first zero of her entire life on an exam. She nearly cried:

— "Why does this lecturer hates me so much?", she whispered to herself before deciding to gain the courage to ask him exactly that...

— "Why did you give me a zero on my paper?"

— "Well, Helen, your results where very poor, even when compared to the rest of the class", the teacher replied.

— "But I worked so hard", she insisted.

— "Well, you might have worked hard, but you understand little", he said.

— "What can I do to improve?", she asked.

— "My best suggestion is for you to choose a rap song, and then practice singing it", he recommended.

Helen was surprised with his answer: — "A rap song? But how is that going to help me improve my ability with speaking, writing and hearing the language?", she asked back.

The teacher looked at her, and answered back: — "Helen, I have plenty of experience and I ask you to trust me. Just choose a song, translate it, and practice singing it every day!"

That day, Helen went to her dorm, picked a song, and sent her choice to him for approval. And when the teacher approved, she was very happy, because it was indeed her favorite song, even though it sounded like something of a poor gueto.

In the following days, Helen used it to gain her language skills by practicing as she was told every single day. And six months later, she was having the best scores in all the papers.

At the end of that academic year, she said to the teacher:

— "Do you know what impressed me the most from my results? It was that I became a better student not only in your classes, but in the classes of all the other teachers."

Helen had just learned a very valuable lesson. She learned that happiness can create miracles. By becoming happier, she actually became a better student on all the classes she attended. That is what the teacher intended for her to see. That is what he was expecting when suggesting that she should learn a language with music. He taught her that success could only be acquired by combining positive emotions with learning.

Helen took those lessons to heart, and kept applying them in all areas of her life, including when choosing a husband. She picked one that would make her smile, as she later told the teacher. Today, Helen is happily married, and has a very fulfilling life to match her constant positive mood.

The Music in Our Soul

Every time Tim arrived home from work, he would hear a strange and creepy music coming from one of his neighbors' apartment. It truly sounded like music from a horror movie, and scared him. He had no idea who was that flutist, until one day, through another neighbor, he met her. Her name was Veronika and she had quite a lot of professional experience as a musician. She seemed very friendly too, to his surprise. And yet, she told him that she didn't have many friends, and invited him for a cup of tea, to know him better, and to which he reluctantly accepted.

During their conversation over a tea she prepared, Tim realized that Veronika didn't have many opportunities in life. Her physical disability made her end up getting rejected in many job interviews she applied to, and despite her college degree in pedagogy.

— "That is sad to know", he added. — "I listened to your songs and can tell that you are very talented", he said, avoiding saying how creepy the choice in songs also was.

— "Thank you! That's very kind of you", she answered.

Right there, Tim got an idea to encourage her:

— "Why don't you transform that passion into a business by teaching others, and even create a music school?"

— "That's a great idea! I never thought about it before. I would consider it", she happily told Tim.

Veronika did gave a lot of thoughts to this idea, and soon after, she took it to heart and opened her own music school with the help of her family.

Today, with dozens of students being trained by this highly skillful woman, she regained her trust in herself. Her success was such, that she had to start hiring more music teachers to work for her. More than that, with her renewed confidence, she also found a man she loves and that appreciates her for who she is, more than her looks. Veronika got married with this musician.

Veronika remains today living in the United States as a very successful businesswoman and music teacher.

The Blessings in Our Life

Garcia was a very depressed individual when he met Robert for the first time, but didn't hide it either. He enjoyed speaking openly to Robert, who was an author. He would tell him about his addiction to alcohol but also the dream of one day write a book about his insights on life. Garcia, however, had difficulties in focusing, on any activity, and his depression made him always end up drunk in the house, singing alone to songs of Elvis Presley, especially at night.

Robert did want to help his new friend, and so told him the following:

— "Why don't you write only one chapter at a time, instead of thinking of a whole book?", he asked.

— "That's a really good idea! I never thought about it before", answered Garcia.

On the following day, Garcia would meet Robert again, this time to tell him about his results.

— "I tried really hard, to put my thoughts together and express some ideas, and do as you said, but couldn't. I think I should just give up."

— "No! Don't do that just yet", insisted Robert. — "Instead of writing about your knowledge, why not write about yourself only, and for now, namely, your thoughts about yourself and your past experiences?"

Garcia looked at Robert with shame.

— "All I have to write on regards to my past is horrible, like my drug addictions, the gang I used to hang out with, and so on."

— "Yes, it might be true, but it is also very true for you; and those experiences can eventually connect into a bigger picture, which will reveal a very interesting book with a better outlook on life."

Garcia took the new challenge. In fact, on the next day he was very different. He went to Robert again, this time with a huge smile on his face, to tell him what happened.

— "You were right! You know, yesterday I was able to start and actually finish a full chapter. Then, I continued, because I couldn't stop myself. I wrote my first book about my latest experiences, plus my past in dealing with drugs, the struggles with my family, and much more. My mind was unstoppable. I just couldn't stop writing. It was as if I had plugged myself to something else beyond my awareness. And you know what else? I am drinking much less and smoking much less as well. I literally forgot time and the need to smoke or drink when I was writing. Thanks to this experience, I was able to realize how my life made me who I am, with all my addictions, and how writing allowed me to rediscover myself. Thank you so much! I have been trying to write my first book for many years, and I am now actually about to start the second, thanks to your suggestions. I never thought about simply writing about my past and my life experience. It has been a wonderful experience and also a very therapeutic one. I feel different and more confident on my future."

Garcia finished and published that book quite fast, and then continued, moving to the next ones. Some of his books were adapted by his brother, who is a film maker, for inspiration. And so, Garcia had just, unexpectedly, turned into, not just an author, but a screenwriter. From that moment on, his life headed on a very different and more fulfilling direction.

The Teacher Who Sacrificed His Career

I rene, a college finalist, was at one point in her life faced with two options: Either she followed one of the teachers against the mainstream and the opinions of others, or she followed everyone else.

She asked him what to do to guarantee a bright future and he blatantly stated:

— "While a student, learn Portuguese, English and Spanish. As a part-time job, work with foreigners from these countries, to practice the languages you are studying. Then, take also businesses classes and whenever possible. And when studying abroad, apply what you learn by creating a small company targeting tourists from your home country or by associating yourself with a local traveling agency and profiting from that business connection."

She did as recommended, and started earning much more as a student than any of her colleagues that had already graduated and were employed in different countries. She even considered quitting college, and said this to her teacher, to which he replied:

— "Persist along this path and graduate first. Your certificate will open doors too. And you will have plenty of opportunities to set your own business."

She followed through and eventually decided to pursue another path, by becoming a manager in the biggest Chinese company — Alibaba. She also became a part-time model. Her teacher, however, was fired for giving advice to students that contradicted absolutely everything that was intended for them, even if Irene ended up becoming the most successful of her class, and the rest of her classmates didn't reach even close to her results. Many of them, dissatisfied with their life, kept changing job and complaining about the low salary they received. But no wonder, for they don't have even half of the worth and life experience that Irene had accumulated while still in college.

The Stranger in the Coffee Shop

Gabriela was still a student who worked part-time as a barista, when she met a stranger who used to sit there, in that coffee shop, to work on his laptop, every single day. He was an entrepreneur who spent all of his time preparing and working on several projects. But he enjoyed talking to Gabriela too, for it was very easy to make her smile.

Feeling confident and very curious, one day Gabriela approached this stranger to ask him what exactly was he doing. And he explained that he already had one online business but was preparing himself for more in order to increase his average monthly revenue.

— "I wish I had something online as well. I hate working here as a waitress", she told him.

— "You can do that!", he replied.

— "But how? I don't even know anything about business", she said desperately.

— "Well, then let us chop that idea into parts first: What can you do? And could it be something that you would do online?", he added.

— "I can be an interpreter, but this job is seasonal and usually doesn't give me much income, not enough to be considered a par-time at least", she argued.

— "Well, then why not be more professional about it? You can create a page on the internet offering your services, and then write a list of things you can do related to it, such as interpretation, translation, voice recording, and much more. Just check what are other people looking for, when they search for translators on the internet!"

She never thought about such options, and decided to follow with his advice. Weeks later she returned to see him:

— "I am quitting my job!", she said quite joyfully.

— "What went wrong?", he asked her worried.

— "Nothing! I simply followed your advice and now I am making lots of money with many clients", she quickly replied with enthusiasm.

She then proceeded to explain how she designed a plan for her online work based on what they talked.

He was very happy for her, and decided to add a new challenge for Gabriela.

— "Why not combine all that and, since your clients are business owners, do a market research for them, by telling them the names of companies that are available to supply their business?"

From that moment on, while her colleagues had to struggle and compete in finding a job, she was actually able to self-employ herself and work at distance from her computer, and with a new idea: to do market research for companies abroad.

Now, the most interesting part of this story, is that she was not the brightest of her class, even though she was the only one that used to spend hours talking to that business owner every time she saw him. She absorbed everything that she heard from him, and lives now a free lifestyle, by traveling the whole world with what she earns while working from her laptop. Gabriela still sends messages to that man who helped her and ended up becoming her best friend. Sometimes, she is sending him messages from Peru, other times from Brazil, China, and many other nations from around the world. Last time she contacted him, Gabriela was sharing her plans to move to Spain and study for a Masters degree there.

The Limits of Faith

James had a very high popularity rate among his college students, which attracted Emily once she heard about this teacher. She was about to participate in a speech competition and needed his help.

— "Well, Emily, I honestly have no idea on how to help you win that competition. I am not an English native speaker, I did not study philosophy in college, and I don't have experience in doing public speeches."

Emily was not expecting this answer, but something within her heart was telling her to trust him, and so she insisted.

— "Maybe we could have a coffee together and talk about it", she added eagerly and calmly while looking at his eyes.

Emily was a very attractive woman and it was hard to say no to her; and so, James agreed to see her later. In fact, he could have easily fallen in love with this student, for she had many rare attributes that are not common to find in one single person: she was smart, kind, attractive, and humble.

During that same evening, they met.

— "I really need to win this competition", she started. And the word need, truly confused James.

— "What would happen if you lose?", he asked back.

— "I can't lose", she said anxiously. — "This competition is very important to me."

— "Well, then it shouldn't be!", he said. — "If a competition is so important to you, is because you're not happy with your life as it is. But you should have other things going on, under your control."

— "Do you have a boyfriend?", James added.

— "No", she told him in shame, while lowering her head down. But she then looked up and into his eyes and said: — "Boys are stupid and I have no patience for them. I don't think they like me either. They always runaway from me!"

— "Maybe you're just too smart and they don't like that", he explained, while realizing that Emily was indeed very mature for her age and seeking validation from him.

— "Yes, they usually want a woman that they can control, and I scare them away", she said with a smile, while feeling properly understood.

— "Well, then maybe you can focus on something else in your life, to gain more joy.", he added. — "Meanwhile, let's see if I can help you", he continued, while looking at the paper she had prepared.

James asked her a few questions about it, and then realized that she didn't really believe in her own words on that paper, but was only trying to win the competition.

— "Look, Emily, if you want me to help you, you will need to be honest."

— "But I will lose if I am honest", she quickly responded.

— "That's the only way I can help you", he said to her.

She paused for a while, and then reluctantly agreed, while assuming that this would most likely make her lose the competition. And when noticing that on her facial expression, James tried to comfort her:

— "An honest truth towards the common good is always far more important than winning at something with a lie."

James then proceeded in teaching Emily on how to combine the values of different cultures, in order to present a speech that shows intelligence as the ability to integrate different perspectives about life. Emily followed his recommendations, changed the whole speech she had prepared in one night, and thinking that she would lose, but then, she actually won. She couldn't hold her happiness and had to tell him.

— "I blindly trusted you, without even knowing why, thinking I would lose, but I won."

After that day, she developed a certain kind of blind faith on this lecturer, and gained more confidence in herself too. She decided to apply for an internship abroad and asked for his help in writing a recommendation letter. And even though knowing that he might not see her again, he didn't want to stop Emily from following her dreams, so he wrote that letter in the best way he could, and she got accepted. They kept in contact, and again, when she decided to apply for a job, she asked for his help. And again, James helped her, by rewriting her Resume and Application Letter. And again, she succeeded. She got the job she wanted.

Emily couldn't be happier and more confident at that point. She was literally getting everything she wanted with the help of this man. And she still couldn't see why.

— "Since I met you, I have trusted in everything you say. And it seems insane, because it contradicts everything else I ever thought and believed, including what everyone tells me that I should be doing. But it works. Every single time, everything you told me, works. I am a much happier and more successful person thanks to you. And it is amazing how you can predict everything so well. You are a great teacher."

What Emily was unable to see is that, the apparently magic powers of James, came from his heart — he was in love with Emily. And she was in love with him too, but too scared to admit it. Her blind faith in him had reached a limit, for the last step would be to blindly fall in love with him and let herself go. And yet, she couldn't give that final step. She was too scared.

They kept in contact when James stoped working as a teacher and changed country. And James did try to see her to confess his love. But Emily was too scared, and all because of a ten years age gap, and the idea that a teacher could not become her lover. This was the only thing that she couldt trust about her heart. And so, she lost the chance to get married to this man and build a family with him. To this day, Emily never found a man she can respect and admire as much as James, and never will. Their relationship was unique and can never be replaced. As the years passed and Emily grew older, she learned another important lesson: whenever you follow your heart, you don't just become successful, but you also find true love.

The Buddhist and the Narcissist

Nicholas was a strong and determined man. At 18yo, he moved from the countryside to a big city in order to pursue his dream of achieving a masters degree. With a personality of steel and without any empathy for others, it was hard for him to maintain any friend. This, until he met Bryan. Bryan was a buddhist, always very patient towards others, always listening to everyone empathically, never reacting to expressions of anger or resentment. And that anger was what kept Nicholas's willpower strong, for he was addicted to bodybuilding and to attracting women that, quite often, were much older and more mature than him. Even one of his female teachers couldn't resist him and eventually became one of his girlfriends.

Nevertheless, Nicholas's personality would always interfere with the outcome of his relationships, which never lated too long. Nicholas was also very narcissistic and selfish, so when Bryan told him that he wanted to write a book with the knowledge he was sharing with others, Nicholas laughed loudly and mocked him during the following days.

After they graduated from college, Nicholas decided to start a business by owning a restaurant and invited Bryan to join him. It was a big challenge for both but their cooperation could lead to a great success. That, if Nicholas had not taken advantage of the humility of Bryan. Nicholas's selfishness and greed took over his mind, and he decided to find a way to expel Bryan from the business in order to keep all the profits for himself.

Bryan was very forgiving of other's ignorance and didn't end the friendship because of this. But karma would eventually catch up with Nicholas, and the business didn't last long before he bankrupted.

Nicholas was still too proud of himself and determined to become rich in a short period of time, even though life had other plans for him and none of his ideas ever worked. Bryan, on the other hand, decided to pursue his passion of embracing others with his faith, and that led him to meet another buddhist — a rich businesswoman with whom he would get married.

She was as much in love with him as with his knowledge, and encouraged Bryan to become her personal business consultant, which allowed her to become ten times richer. Together, they were able to become multimillionaires and develop an international network of business partners. And those partners would always seek Bryan for insights on how to improve and become wealthier, which reverted back in the form of more profit for everyone.

Nearly ten years had passed, and Bryan decided to search for his friend, Nicholas, to see how he was doing. But nothing would have made him prepared for what he witnessed. Nicholas's personality, over time, made him lose every single job and relationship he had, until he found himself alone and unemployed, living from welfare. He then developed chronic depression and started having hallucinations, which forced him to be on antidepressants on a regular basis, to hold on to his life and avoid committing suicide. After a few more years like this, Nicholas's last stop was at a psychiatric hospital.

Bryan was still willing to help his friend and suggested that he should leave that hospital to live with him for a while and try a fresh restart. But Nicholas, now with a stronger ego than ever before, resented this offer profoundly, felt an overwhelming fire of hate and jealousy coming from within, and brutally replied:

— "I do whatever I want with my life, including taking antidepressants and remaining in this hospital forever if I want to. And this is my choice, not yours, so you have no right whatsoever to tell me what to do. And you can also disappear, because I don't need to see you ever again."

After hearing these violent words, Bryan realized that he would never be able to help his friend again, who would most likely die soon. Months later after receiving Bryan's visit, Nicholas decided to signup for an electroconvulsive therapeutical treatment. It did not end well.

The Meaning of Life

Fred and Justin were in their third year of college when they met for the first time. They had both been invited to do a speech for the freshmen about how to adapt to their new lifestyle. Fred had been selected because he was the most popular and brightest student from the department of psychology, while Justin was chosen by accident, after a student from the department of education quitted at the last minute.

Their speech was impressive in different ways. Fred talked about the difficulties that students often face and Justin focused on the solutions to any problem, which he applied himself to overcome his own struggles. Both presentations appeared helpful to the students, but although Fred didn't gain much from the experience, Justin, who up until that moment was barely known to anyone, suddenly became very popular.

In the following days, Fred and Justin maintained their friendship and continued their conversations. They had different viewpoints on life but could somehow interconnect them. As time went by, it became obvious why they were so different, for Fred came from a wealthy family while Justin was poor and struggled with financial difficulties. Their encounters always ended in the same way, as Fred insisted that the only way to enjoy life is by openly talking about the things that nobody notices, such as the stars, the illogical thinking of the poor, the advantages of the existence of mental illnesses, and so on, while Justin, on the other hand, had a more conservative approach, based on his religious background, and strong convictions on the ground that the only way to live life properly consists on helping others with theirs and in making efforts to change ourselves as much as possible along the way.

Their conversations were as exciting for those listening as they were confusing, because, among so many contradictions, nothing could explain why these two individuals kept talking to one another. Their friendship became more interesting in time, as they both started working together as members of the students' union. They shared responsibilities but Justin was the one taking it more seriously, and arranging many meetings in which he would confront teachers with their policies and behaviors inside the classroom. This bold attitude would, as a matter of fact, cost him his reputation and grades. Fred didn't seem to show any interest about the students' issues and preferred to spend his time sharing insights with the professors, which often agreed with his words.

Despite these different approaches, Justin and Fred kept meeting each other regularly to discuss a variety of topics. The conversations typically lasted hours in a complete disagreement. One of the most interesting talks they ever had, was about the meaning of life. Justin would claim that the purpose of life is to be happy and help others, while Fred believed that happiness is an illusion and it is much easier to give antidepressants to people than to teach them how to be happy.

— "I believe there's knowledge and potential in anyone to improve, including among the poorest", Justin argued. But Fred disagreed.

— "Poor people can't learn anything and you're being delusional about this issue."

— "I can give you a good example", Justin added. — "Helping students is a very good way for them to change something in their academic life, which will then allow them to help themselves and others that will come later."

Fred was shaking his head in complete disagreement as Justin spoke.

— "Those changes won't last long and students will never appreciate your efforts", he added.

Their lack of cooperation towards the same goals led to an increasing feeling of frustration and stress in Justin that was noticing that he was talking alone, and so he left the student's union. Justin then went back to being a discreet and unknown individual inside the campus, and Fred remained known as a confident, gentle, pleasant, joyful and an excellent knower of the expensive pleasures of traveling to amazing cities. Even his choice of words was always rich. Nobody was ever able to explain the friendship of such different souls. Was the end of their conversations something normal and truly expectable? Or was there a different meaning to their encounters? It was one o'clock of the most beautiful winter night when Fred called every single one of his friends to talk about the stars and how much he appreciated their companionship. When the last call ended, Fred contemplated the stars for a little longer and last time. Then, after opening his harms on the top of the building, Fred decided to become another star in the sky, and jumped to his death.

That night, Fred had called everyone except Justin. Fred was convinced that life had no meaning and a disagreement about it wasn't something he was willing to face. The violent impact of his body on the ground seemed far more realistic at that point. Fred soul eventually visited every single one of his friends, leaving Justin for last. But it was this last visit that made him realize what he had lost, for Justin was still struggling but never giving up on life. He eventually became a self-employed nomad, and traveled the world, discovering everything it has to offer.

The Cost of Jealousy

Rachel has always been a very confident and lucky woman since a very early age. Thanks to her older brother, she was able to avoid most problems that people typically face throughout life. Her brother was also her idol and helped her overcome many obstacles, really any kind that she could find. The fact that he worked as a professional fortuneteller with cartomancy allowed Rachel to escape any negative outcomes in her life or to simply be prepared for them. Thanks to his abilities, his sister was always ready for anything that could ever happen. He would even constantly call her to make sure that she was doing well in life. Thanks to her brother, Rachel was able to prevent accidents, threats and even develop a deeper sense of spirituality. The strong protection of her brother, this earthly angel in her life, helped her for a very long time, and so much that she eventually became a very successful physician in a famous hospital. She used to say to her friends that her brother was like her private angel.

Everything drastically changed when her brother suddenly started making a lot of money and gaining popularity with his newly found spiritual group. Rachel became extremely jealous of his success and of his followers too. After realizing that her brother was now available for so many more people, which would benefit from the same she did for a very long time, Rachel didn't feel special anymore. She felt betrayed and resentful. And, out of revenge, she stopped talking to him and started spreading false negative rumors about him — gossips depicting him as an evil and mad man with schizophrenic tendencies.

Upon acknowledging that his sister wasn't talking to him anymore but merely hating him and replying to him with bitterness and offenses, while spreading vicious rumors to destroy his image behind his back, this fortuneteller felt deeply offended and had no other choice but to avoid her and stop tormenting himself with her actions. He never again contacted her or tried to know about her life.

One day, Rachel decided to change job and move to another country in order to make much more money than him, and to reestablish her own pride on herself. She moved to the middle-east, knowing that she would become very rich in a short period of time thanks to the salary offered. But, instead, Rachel ended up paying at once for a full life of bad karma that she was avoiding, as well as the positive outcomes that she was ungrateful for, when a terrorist attack made a bomb explode in the same section of the hospital where she was working. She died instantly.

The Man with a Dream

David was born in a poor family of rude and reckless parents, and since a very early age that he heard from them, and in a regular basis, things like:

— "Money doesn't grow on trees";

— "The only way to become rich is by stealing from others";

— "You need to lie to become rich";

— "You have to do something illegal in order to make real money";

— "Only hard work and total commitment to the system, and blind obedience to a boss can allow you to have a normal life";

— "Always obey and never react".

Every single time he failed in following these rules, his mother would shout, call him insane, stupid, lunatic and neurotic. His father, on the other hand, would slap his face so hard, that his head would sometimes bounce against the wall and bleed for hours. A shout from any of his parents typical meant pain almost immediately. And so, like a well-trained monkey, David allowed these messages to become part of his subconscious mind.

His persistence as a student eventually got him to college, but after graduation, he tried to follow what he was programmed to do and, job after job, no matter how hard he tried, or how high he was in the company's hierarchy, he always ended up being fired. And so, many years later, alone and depressed, David eventually concluded that his life was miserable and the strong discipline received at home had to be wrong. But would it be too late for him to change? He seemed to struggle with it. The words he received had now become an overwhelming component of his daily thoughts. At thirty years old, David was sleeping an average of three hours a day and working more than twelve hours from Monday to Sunday in multiple jobs. When health started failing on him and he couldn't continue any longer with this lifestyle, he had to make a choice. He realized that if this is the meaning of being normal, then being abnormal should probably be better.

In the following days, David searched for photos of trees without leaves inside magazines. Then, he glued small notes of money that he had cut to them. That final image made him feel happy for the first time in many years. So, he decided to quit every single one of the many jobs he had, in order to become a security guard and contemplate his work every day.

During the night shifts and at home too, David would stare at those images and dream about a life that he couldn't get. As his parents had taught him to always work harder and never say no to authority, he was the only one always working extra hours but also during holidays and Christmas. He never said no to anyone. But his money tree seemed to make him happy and help him endure his misery.

It was during a Christmas night, that two drunk men entered his workplace and stabbed him to death, ending is suffering.

In the morning of his funeral, his mobile was ringing. It was the bank, trying to reach him to offer a special promotional loan of five thousand dollars, which would have allowed David to follow his dream of buying a plane ticket to travel abroad and then become an English teacher in The Phillipines. David also never found that his mother was taking antidepressants in a regular basis and that his father had spent three years of his youth in a mental hospital. His parents were indeed wrong about many things because they were mentally ill. But poor David never realized it and paid the ultimate price of obeying the wrong people with his own life.

The Teenager Who Loved to Read

Jack was a very shy teenager, and for this very reason, constantly bullied by his classmates too. The fear and stress led him to a depression that would affect his school grades. The fact that he was studying in a school with very bad reputation didn't help either. And because he had to always be alone, without friends, Jack would spend most of his time in the local library, hidden in a corner, reading books. It was during those moments that he eventually started reading encyclopedias on psychology and psychiatry, and more precisely, on the topics of intelligence, communication and mind control. He become fascinated and obsessed with everything related to the brain.

Jack ended up realizing that he had the power to shift his whole reality, by changing himself and the way he interacted with others. That confidence made him feel that life was not as overwhelming as he had previously assumed. The more he would read, the more curious he would become, and the faster he would assimilate the knowledge and move on to the following encyclopedia. In a few months, Jack had already read over one hundred books and encyclopedias from different local libraries and on a huge variety of subjects. And when that wasn't enough, he decided to search for books in other libraries, by traveling more to other cities to get unique books. He also searched for more updated content in different bookstores. Jack was even saving the money his parents gave him for lunch to buy more books, on relationships, communication, emotions, and so on. He was fascinated with everything related to the human mind. But he didn't want his parents to know that he was spending his lunch money on books, so he was donating his books after finishing reading them to local libraries.

The books were changing him. In a short period of time, nobody could believe how confident he had become, how smart he was now, and how quick he was to make judgments and control the behaviors of others over him. He even started reading about martial arts to be able to face his bullies. At one point, nobody dared confronting him as before.

When time wasn't enough for so much reading, Jack started sacrificing his own sleep, just to stay all night long hooked on a book he loved. All that knowledge would eventually pay off. Years later, Jack became a successful College Professor and married the woman of his dreams, a beautiful college student he had met when visiting a Polish library.

The Fighter with a Heart of Gold

Tom was a skinny boy growing up in a poor and violent neighborhood. Unluckily for him, his parents got very poor after his mother lost her job and he had to move to a poorer city. In that city, Tom learned the meaning of fear. Every day, he would be either robbed or beaten to the ground, and it was so normal that it felt kind of strange whenever a day would pass and none of these things would happen. In order to avoid these situations, Tom had to start checking for alternative paths to return home and go to school. Many times, his walk home would double or triple in time just for him to avoid the bullies. He would then arrive to his room and lay down in bed, depressed, thinking about his day, and wondering about the meaning of life. Life had really little meaning to him. Girls wouldn't even look at him, except to laugh or feel pity. And at some point, started getting difficult to justify to his parents where were his scars coming from. His mother believed he was just clumsy and stupid and his father didn't have a different opinion. But one day he surprised everyone at home, when he said to his parents at the dinner table: — "I want to learn Karate."

They paused for a moment to consider what they had just heard.

— "Are you serious?", his mother asked, while laughing.

— "Look at how skinny and fragile you are!", his father added. — "You can't even kill a mosquito, much less fight anyone."

— "I'm not going to waste my money on you, to then see you coming home crying because apart from being beaten at school, now you are beaten at a gym as well. Fighting isn't for you. You better take that out of your mind", his mother added.

His father looked at him with shame: — "You should go to the army. That's where you really get your training. You can't handle Karate."

— "But some of my friends are practicing it", Tom insisted, in another attempt at getting their approval.

— "Just look!", his father shouted while waving his hand at Tom. — "You are even afraid to be slapped, and you want to learn Karate? Grow up!"

Tom turned his head down in shame and his father grabbed his shoulder, while shouting closer to his hear: — "I should be the one learning karate, not you. Look at yourself!"

— "Enough", said his mother. — "Don't humiliate him any further. I think he understood".

Tom had his eyes on the table, feeling embarrassed, and his mother, to compensate for the situation, told him: — "Maybe you can take swimming classes. You have back problems and it would be good for you. I've been taking them and I feel much better with myself."

— Sure!", said Tom, seeking for a chance to meet new friends that didn't know he was being bullied.

In the following day, Tom went to the gym to subscribe to the swimming classes. When he was looking at the subscription paper, he noticed that everything had the same price, and the difference was just an X. And so, he proceeded to confirm:

— "Is Karate and swimming under the same price and in the same days of the week?"

— "Yes, you can either pick one or the other, but it's just a cross on paper actually. Some people even start one and then choose the other", the receptionist confirmed.

— "Does that mean I can change after one month?", Tom anxiously asked.

— "Sure, you can change without any extra fees whenever you want", she told him.

Happily, Tom went for a month to his swimming lessons, to please his parents, and whenever that was over, he would take a shower, get dressed, and run to the other section, where Karate was taking place. He was astonished, at the discipline, the commitment, the beautiful techniques, the meditation process, the coordination, and even the instructor shouting at the class, which for him sounded motivational. And well, Tom did change his classes. His parents thought he was still taking swimming lessons and would ask him every night how was everything going, but Tom was lying, because he had started Karate. And it was in Karate that Tom learned how to meditate, which he practiced every morning at home, and every night before sleeping. He would close the door of his room, and when nobody was watching, he would meditate for at least thirty minutes. If that wasn't possible, he would get out of bed, when everyone was asleep, to meditate in the dark.

He was so fascinated with Karate, that he kept practicing the techniques at home, and for hours sometimes. And yet, that wasn't enough, for Tom had now more courage but was still getting beaten by bullies. And he didn't know what to do at this point, why he was braver than before, learning Karate, doing more exercises and still getting beaten. But it all changed when, one day, on his way to school, he saw an advertisement promoting Muay Thai classes in his hometown, a super cool poster with the instructor doing a spinning kick in the air. Tom just couldn't lose that chance, for he was now fascinated to learn this new martial art. He quitted his Karate classes and started practicing Muay Thai, and his body quickly begun to change with that hard training; he started growing muscles all over his body, and was much calmer than before, because he was fighting with others in every single class.

One by one, he started beating all of his bullies, and easily. Many times, he didn't even have to fight them. He would merely swipe their leg to make them fall on the ground, or grab them in the air and throw them easily on the floor. And despite his attackers being bigger and heavier than him, he would actually be gentle, not to hurt them. Because Tom wasn't really into hurting other people. He was into peace and harmony, and meditation was giving him that chance to know himself more, while Muay Thai was showing him that he could defeat men much bigger than him just by using technique and strategy.

The news spread fast in his school and neighborhood, and soon enough everyone was afraid to fight him. Sometimes, they only had to look at his eyes, to say: — "Sorry for what I said and did; I don't want to fight you".

Interestingly, Tom didn't want to fight anyone either. He was simply not afraid of it anymore, and knew he could easily beat anyone, or at least confront without the fear of getting hurt. He knew well what it meant to be punched and kicked in the head and wasn't afraid of it any longer. And so, he became so popular, for his skills, that his previous bullies feared him, and other bullies worshipped him. Tom soon started being invited to join gangs, to create fights on purpose, and started drinking too, and a lot, when with those groups.

One day, at the beach with his gang of friends and other people they met, he saw a beautiful girl, and really liked her a lot. He went to her to talk to her, but she replied him:

— "Aren't you Tom, that guy that beats others all the time just for fun?"

— "Yeah, that's me!", he answered while laughing with a cocky smile.

— "Well, you see, I don't like bullies, I don't like people like you, so please go away", she told him.

He was devastated, but that's when he realized what he had become. He had become what he despised the most. In his journey to protect himself, he had become like his enemies. And he couldn't get anyone to love him, not even a girl. People were just and simply afraid of him. That night, Tom felt empty and lonely, and realized that most people are just cowards. They will bully the weak, until the weak get strong, but then all they get is respect by fear. Indeed, people only respect what they fear. But that's also when Tom realized that his mates weren't really his true friends. In the following day, Tom went to a church in search for answers, and met a young girl there that invited him to join their group. Tom went to their meetings, and for the first time he felt loved, for the first time he realized what real love is. He didn't really feel comfortable with the singing, but loved this group of friendly christians, and felt respected in a different way, in a loving way. From that moment on, Tom dedicated himself to understanding that type of love. Instead of the emptiness of his meditation, and the courage of the fighting, Tom found himself searching for love in a christian form. He realized that he didn't have it, never felt it before, and was actually empty inside. That's when embraced Jesus Christ's words and God in his heart.

Tom then continued in this path, and today he is loved by many that can feel his warmth. Many can now feel the love in his heart, for he knows that humans are weak, and speaks to their heart in the meetings, to embrace them with compassion and pass courage with his words and speeches. Tom learned the meaning of building a strong heart and the importance it has. His mission in life now is to bring this courage to others, so that they can feel it from within. And that girl, who had invited him to join their group, couldn't be more proud of him, for Tom had become the man she always wanted — a man with a beautiful heart. She was actually the one proposing marriage to him after only a couple of months of being in a relationship with him had passed, because she didn't want to lose him, or allow any traditions to be on the way of their future.

The Self-Made DJ

Phillip didn't really know what electronic music was until one day, when he was 16yo, one of his friends showed it at his place. He was astonished, because, you see, Phillip was a typical geek, always talking about strange things, like UFOs and his imaginary dreams about life, and so, nobody took him seriously when he later said that he would like to learn how to DJ for a radio. Many even laughed at him. He tried to talk to some of his friends that worked on the school's radio, asking them for an opportunity to choose songs and work with them, but they refused. His parents, also never allowed him to go clubbing at night. But that didn't stop Phillip. He started searching for electronic music online, and then, he would combine them together, mix and remix them with his computer, to create his own DJ sets. He was really good at it, and proud of his results, but still nobody took him seriously. And not even when his mixes were good enough to be praised, would people believed he had done them by himself. Everyone was closing the doors on him, and not letting him perform in a club or bar either; even the smallest and crappiest ones refused him. Phillip never got even a single chance; not until one day, when he met Sam, a part-time DJ, during his job at a sales company. Sam said he was there just to make some pocket money until he could find a better job, but would like to share his work with Phillip. Thanks to Sam, Phillip got a chance to see how DJs really work. Sam took him to his house, and then invited friends for a small gathering in his garage. The sound speakers were huge, and they immediately started playing hard techno and dancing to it. Phillip was fascinated, like a small child in front of a carousel.

— "Come here! Look! I will show you how it works and how to perform live!", Sam told him.

Sam then showed him how he uses a DJ table, how he mixes the music, and how he selects it. Sam tough him everything he knew, and soon, Phillip was having fun as well, mixing their music. Sam even mixed some of Phillip's tracks to show him how cool his selection was. And well, that experience had just excited Phillip even more. Now, he was dreaming every night before falling sleep, imagining himself DJing for thousands of people. That opportunity was still being rejected to him. But one day he an idea: He would instead organize parties for other Djs like Sam and his friends. He went to several clubs and finally found one that liked the idea. He then posted an ad online searching for more DJs, and got dozens of applications. He selected the ones he believed to be the best, to join him and Sam, and at the end of the flyer, he basically put himself on the list, in small letters. From the many DJs he invited, he was actually one of them.

Those parties that he organized were a huge success, and to everyone's surprise, Phillip's first performances were actually outstanding, when compared to others, and surpassed the attention all the others DJs where getting. As matter of fact, for the following days, nobody could stop talking about Phillip. He became very famous with his first performances. And from that point on, he kept being invited for more and more parties, organized by others. Soon, Phillip was performing every single week, sometimes two times or three times a week.

In less than a year, Phillip became the most popular and famous DJs in his whole country. And yes, he still looked like a geek, but his rave parties were the most amazing everyone had ever seen. And he started getting requests to play in many other countries as well, eventually even winning world competitions as a DJ and music producer. Today, Phillip is a very famous and well-paid professional DJ, and travels the world to perform for crowds with thousands of people.

The Boy who Talked to Angels

Robert still remembers clearly when one night, as he was in bed, his parents were arguing with one another.

— "Your son is not normal, he is not a normal boy, and you have to accept this fact", said his mother to the father.

— "What do you mean by 'he is not normal'?", the father asked.

— "Your son is retarded. Can't you see that?", she shouts in despair.

Robert started crying while hearing this between walls. He was only 10yo, but that was the first time he heard his parents claiming that he was mentally incapable. Until then, he didn't really know what that meant. He thought that he just had some problems in learning and studying, in understanding other children; he believed he was simply different, and didn't know he was actually inferior to other children, incomplete and abnormal when compared to them.

Robert spent the following weeks on his own, looking through the window of his house, seeing other children outside, playing and screaming at one another with joy. He was observing them and thinking to himself: "What do they have that I don't? Why am I different? And why can't they accept me?"

He noticed that his mother was also talking differently to him and his sister. She would often pet his head, and say: — "It's ok son, you don't have to struggle to be better, because you're not like other children".

Robert knew what this phrase meant. He knew that his parents believed he was inferior and incapable of leading a normal life. He knew he was different in a very negative way. And he did feel very sorry for himself, for not having the same opportunities of other children, to a normal job, a family of his own, etc. When the other kids started growing up and realizing the differences between him and them, they started making fun of him, and ignoring him. Many times, he was the only one who wasn't invited to birthday parties, the only one who wasn't invited to the swimming pool, the beach, school parties, and so on. And after a while, he got used to it, he got accustomed to not being invited anywhere. Whenever he saw his friends debating an event or party, he knew he wouldn't be invited. Occasionally someone would invite him, but someone else would immediately interfere: — "Are you crazy? What are you doing?"

And upon hearing this, Robert would always interfere by saying: — "It's ok; I didn't really want to go anyway".

He knew that everyone saw him as retarded and he learned to accept that he was different, that he wasn't like others. Many times he thought about committing suicide. But one day, when about to do it, he thought to himself: "What do I have to lose if I actually live?"

Well, he didn't really have anything to lose. He had lost everything already, including self-respect. And that's when he decided to read books just for fun. He eventually got excited with so much reading, and also started writing about his own thoughts, his opinions about other people, what he saw in the world, and what he thought about human beings. At the time, Robert didn't really know what was the meaning of channeling. He got to understand that later. For the time being, he simply realized that alone, in his thoughts, he could talk to angels. Meanwhile, his mother got scared, as she could see him sometimes talking alone, and then writing many notes while doing that. She saw those notes, full of phrases and words, and confused, she assumed he was getting worse, insane, autistic, or maybe even schizophrenic and psychopathic. And so, after talking to a psychiatrist that confirmed the gravity of his mental state, she decided to put him in a mental hospital.

When that day came, and before she succeeded, Robert runaway from home. He asked one of his friends that had a car for a ride to the train station, not telling him exactly why he needed it, as he knew his friend wouldn't understand, and took with him only a few clothes and an old computer. For the following years, Robert lived alone in a very poor and old small house. The rent was very cheap, the cheapest he could find in a very old part of the city, even though there were always bugs and cockroaches all over the place. He took every job he could find to be able to pay the rent, and never gave up on trying new opportunities. Many people rejected him, but one part-time after another, he eventually found his way to earn enough money to pay for rent and food. The jobs were badly paid, but he was able to find work in a canteen of an orphanage, serving food to children and teenagers, then some others in callcenters. And well, he was always being humiliated and bullied by his superiors, who didn't respect him, sometimes even by his colleagues, and he lost many jobs as well because people didn't like him and would spread rumors to try to expel him. But he didn't quit and never complained. He kept working hard and as much as he could.

Robert didn't have friends either, but felt at peace with himself, when reading in a garden, in the weekends. And that's when he decided to compile his channeled notes and put them into books. One book after another, he reached hundreds of them. And then, he saw that people all over the world where interested in reading and buying his books. His sales picked up very fast, and at one point, he was able to quit all of his jobs to live as a full-time author. Then, the profit kept increasing, which allowed him to decide to travel around the world. That past had stayed behind him. He was able to finally find peace and happiness as himself. He was also now earning much more money sleeping than he ever did with all of his jobs combined.

When he finally had his own family, after marrying a very carrying woman, he used to tell his wife and his very intelligent children: — "I wish I had a family like ours."

They were never able to understand his past, because for them, he was the brightest, wisest and most caring man they ever met.

The Businessman and the Gold Digger

Mark was constantly going out at night to socialize with people and make new friends, because, as an online business owner, he was spending too many hours alone during the day. It was during one of these moments that he met Victoria. She was the most beautiful girl he had ever seen in a long time and with lots of admirers always surrounding her, trying to gain her approval.

Mark moved in with caution. And when realizing that she was narcissistic, he tried a new approach, which was to basically tease her. Whenever they met, he would make fun of her shoes or her clothes, which irritated her quite a lot, while also triggering her interest in him. After all, he was acting totally different from other guys, and she was curious about the why. That's what Mark wanted. They soon started to date and didn't took long before Mark could steal a kiss from her. The relationship seemed to be going great, until Mark realized that Victoria was always circling around the same topics:

— "How much money did you make last moth?"
— "I think you should buy us a house."
— "Would you offer me a car for my birthday?"
— "When will you offer me a gold ring?"
— "If we get married, would you let me quit my job?"
— "Will you buy us a trip to the Maldives?"

Quite simply, Victoria was a gold digger, and interested only on what Mark had to offer her. And yet, because he was in love, he ignored the red flags and promised her a wedding. He also told her that she could indeed quit her job for them to spend more time together and travel the world.

In order to make Victoria's dreams come true, Mark was now spending many more hours in front of his computer, and less with her. And she resented that, complained that their life was boring, and he was always working, and not giving her any attention whatsoever. She also complained that he wasn't taking her out for dinner as before, but always, always, working.

— "I need to work very hard, so that I can give you what you want", he explained to her.

Victoria didn't seem to understand. She was impatient. And then started to complain that Mark was getting too fat for working too many hours in front of his computer. Eventually, she also started going out more often with her friends, and clubbing without him, flirting with other men too. And Mark, afraid to lose her, tried to prohibit her from drinking and partying with others. But her friends told Victoria that Mark was too ugly and not rich enough for her, and she could easily find better. And so, Victoria decided to follow her friends' words, and leave the relationship to search for a new man that could provide her what she wanted. In time, she found one, a young lawyer, and told Mark, which devastated him, after years investing on their future. But in less than two months of using her for sex, her new toy would leave her, for he realized that she was only interested in his money and was a selfish woman, with nothing more to offer than her own body.

Mark, on the other hand, found a woman that wasn't interested in his superficial achievements but internal. This new woman in his life, fell in love with his kindness, talents and strong personality. And because she was a fitness instructor, she invested her time on him, to help him get in shape and achieve his dreams. Mark became more handsome and richer too.

One day, Victoria was scrolling through social media, when she found their photo. She was shocked, for Mark now looked much better than before, more fit, and was next to a very sexy woman, much more good looking than Victoria ever was.

As Victoria was never able to find a man who would love her as much as Mark did, she came to the realization that true love is not in what you get, but what you appreciate and give to the one you truly want to live the rest of your life with, either during the best or worse moments. In fact, never again did Victoria found a man who would do that for her, who would do so much as Mark did. She did understood her lesson, but never, for the rest of her life, found such as great man as Mark was. Her loss was another woman's luck.

The Student of His Enemy

One night, Tony met Agata and Ruth in a bar and started a conversation with them. He was actually more interested in Agata than Ruth, but kept inviting both out, to different events, in order to spend more time with Agata. In the following nights, Tony was picking up Agata in his car and driving her home, offering her beers, and everything else she would ask for. Tony didn't mind. He wanted to spend as much time as possible with her, because he was falling in love.

This situation continued for a very long time, as Agata was single but sleeping with other guys behind Tony's back, and Tony never really tried to kiss her or formalize any type of relationship with her. He was trying to gain time into her heart.

It all changed for him, when one day he saw her holding hands with another man. That's when he realized he had lost her, even though he never really had her. Tony spent the following nights thinking about it, about what he could have done wrong, and making himself drunk to forget the woman he had just lost to some stranger coming out of nowhere. Then, he realized something: He couldn't get Agata back or understand why she chose this new man, but maybe he could teach him something he should be learning. And so, Tony decided to contact him:

— "I hope everything is going great between the two of you. I was just wondering, if there is any book you can recommend me to read about dating."

— "Sure, I can send you a few that will help you with women", he replied Tony.

In the following weeks, Tony religiously read, every single day, the books that he had received. And in less than one month, he was finally in a relationship. That relationship lasted long enough for Tony to see the end of the relationship of Agata with that guy and many others she met afterwards. And this led Tony to realize something very important: He lost a woman that wasn't meant for him, but gained a friend that would change his whole life. If he had succumbed to the pain of losing that woman, and resented the man that took her from him, he would have never learned the lessons that allowed him to find a woman who truly loves him and isn't just taking advantage of his kindness. By overcoming his loss, he gained something greater than what he ever had: true love.

Book Review Request

Dear Reader, Thank you for purchasing this book! I would love to know your opinion. Writing a book review helps in understanding readers and also has an impact on other reader's purchasing decisions. Your opinion matters. Please write a book review! Your kindness is greatly appreciated!

Booklist

Books written by the author:

Agne: Inside the Mind of a Narcissist

Destiny: When Your Soulmate Finds You

Disenchanted: Poems by Rowan Knight

Illusion: When a Nymphomaniac Falls in Love

One Chance: 20 Short Stories with a Plot Twist and Moral Lesson

Prophecy: A Message to Humanity

Slave: Fulfilling a Prophecy

Soulless: Letters to a Narcissist

About the Publisher

This book was published by the 22 Lions Bookstore.
For more books like this visit www.22Lions.com.
Join us on social media at:
Fb.com/22Lions;
Twitter.com/22lionsbookshop;
Instagram.com/22lionsbookshop;
Pinterest.com/22LionsBookshop.